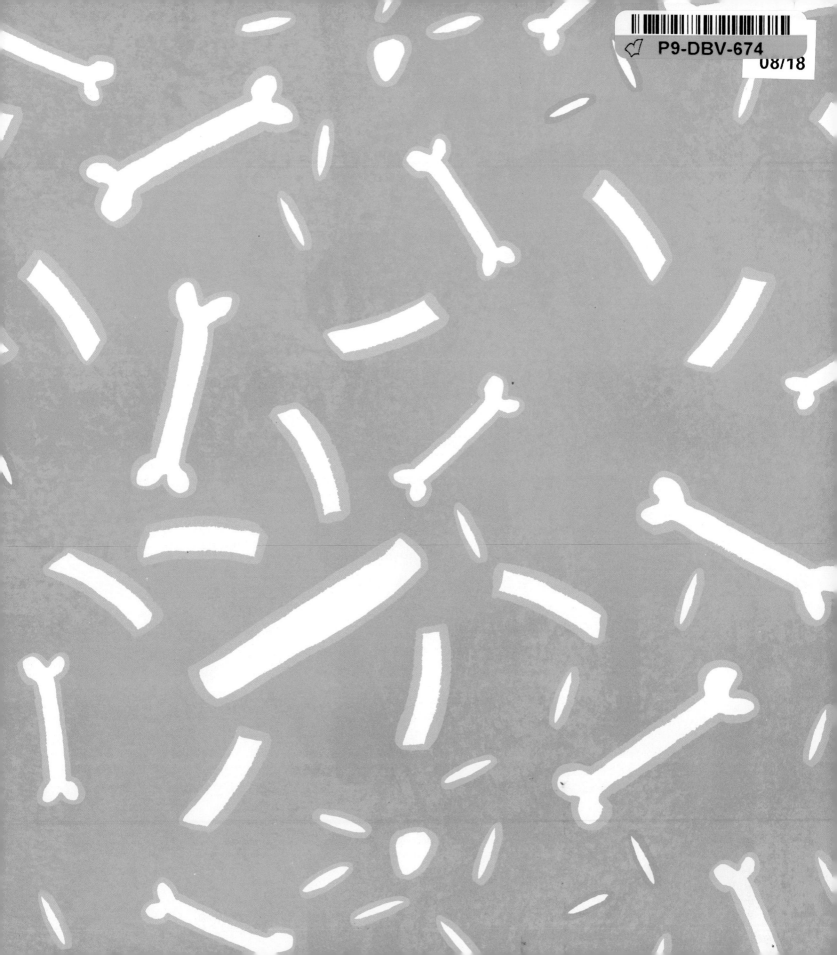

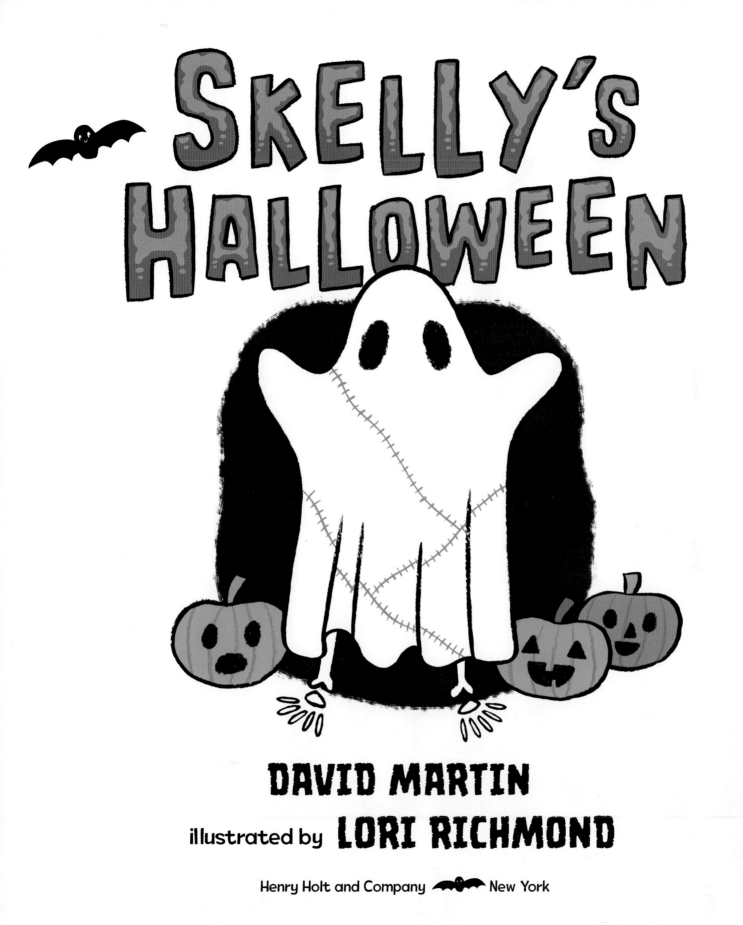

SKELLY'S HALLOWEEN

DAVID MARTIN

illustrated by LORI RICHMOND

Henry Holt and Company 🦇 New York

FOR GRAHAM, WHO WANTED A SKELETON BOOK
—D. M.

FOR LORI K., WHO KEEPS ME TOGETHER
—L. R.

Henry Holt and Company, *Publishers since 1866*
Henry Holt® is a registered trademark of Macmillan Publishing Group, LLC
175 Fifth Avenue, New York, NY 10010 · mackids.com

Library of Congress Cataloging-in-Publication Data

Names: Martin, David, 1944- author. | Richmond, Lori, illustrator.
Title: Skelly's Halloween / David Martin ; pictures by Lori Richmond.
Description: First edition. | New York : Henry Holt and Company, 2018. |
Summary: When a fall causes Skelly B. Skeleton to come apart on Halloween,
his animal friends try to put him back together based on their own bodies.
Identifiers: LCCN 2017041227 | ISBN 9781250127068 (hardcover)
Subjects: | CYAC: Skeleton—Fiction. | Bones—Fiction. | Animals—Fiction. |
Halloween—Fiction. | Humorous stories.
Classification: LCC PZ7.M356817 Ske 2018 | DDC [E]—dc23
LC record available at https://lccn.loc.gov/2017041227

Our books may be purchased in bulk for promotional, educational, or business use.
Please contact your local bookseller or the Macmillan Corporate and Premium Sales Department
at (800) 221-7945 ext. 5442 or by e-mail at MacmillanSpecialMarkets@macmillan.com.

First edition, 2018 / Designed by April Ward
The illustrations for this book were created with pen and ink, foam stamps, and Adobe Photoshop.

Printed in China by RR Donnelley Asia Printing Solutions Ltd., Dongguan City, Guangdong Province
1 3 5 7 9 10 8 6 4 2

"Snap my fingers and rattle my bones— it's Halloween!" said Skelly Bones Skeleton.

And he danced around the room singing,

"Head and shoulders, knees and toes.
Trick-or-treating, here we goes!"

But Skelly had been sleeping all year, because that's what skeletons do when it's not Halloween, so he had to think fast and make a costume.

I don't want to be a witch again. I kept falling off my broomstick.

And when I was a monster, I was so scary I had to hide from myself. And then I didn't get any candy.

"I know! I'll be a ghost."

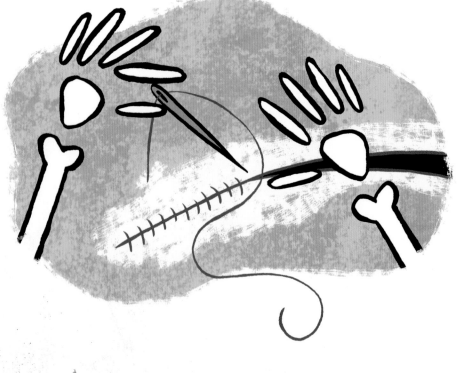

He grabbed a sheet
off his bed, and as fast
as his bony fingers could
cut and sew, Skelly made
a ghost costume.

"Hot diggity.
I am one BOOOO-tiful ghost."

But guess what? When Skelly stepped outside, the wind swept him up into the air and flew him like a kite.

He twirled.

He flipped.

He spun.

Until—OH NO!—
the wind stopped,
and Skelly fell
down,
down,
down.

CRASH!

Luckily, when Skelly hit the ground, he didn't break any bones. But he sure was in pieces.

Legs, ribs, arms, fingers, toes, and all the bones in between were scattered here, there, everywhere.

"Oh my! How am I going to get put back together in time to go trick-or-treating?" said Skelly.

Just then, a snake slithered by. "Snake, I'm so glad to see you," said Skelly. "I need help. Can you give me a hand?"

"A hand? That'sssss a joke, yessss?" said Snake. "But I can help." And bone by bone, he attached this bone to that bone and that bone to this bone.

When Snake was done, Skelly
looked at himself all the way
down to the tip of his tail.

"Wait a minute. I'm not supposed to have a tail. Thank you, Snake. But this isn't me."

"Ssssorry, Sssskelly,"

said Snake.

"We'll fix you," said an ant.

And like a construction team, the whole ant colony got to work.

"Thanks," said Skelly, "but I can't walk with six legs. I keep tripping. I'm a two-legged skeleton."

"We don't understand how we walk with so many legs, either," said an ant.

"I've got two legs. Let me help," said a chicken.

"Oh brother! Now I look like I'm supposed to lay an egg," said Skelly, who was so upset . . .

. . . he collapsed into a pile of bones.

"I'm like Humpty Dumpty," he sighed.
"No one can put me together again.
No more running. No more dancing.

NO MORE TRICK-OR-TREATING!"

Just then, some children found Skelly.
"Look!" whispered the chef. "Bones! Real bones! Let's get out of here!"

"Wait!" said Skelly.

"Don't go. Please. I need help," said Skelly. "I'm not just a pile of bones. I'm a walkin', talkin', trick-or-treatin' Halloween skeleton."

"What happened?" asked the pirate.

"It's a long story. Can you help put me back together the right way?"

"That's easy. We'll make you look just like me.
I'm a walkin', talkin', trick-or-treatin' skeleton too,"
said the girl dressed like a skeleton.

Soon Skelly was Skelly again.
"Click my heels and rattle my bones,"
he said, "I feel like my old self. I can run.
I can jump!"
"And you can go trick-or-treating,"
said the chef.

"I can, indeed. And I know the best places," said Skelly. "Come on, everyone. It's Halloween! And you know what I always say?"

"Sure," they shouted. "Trick or treat, smell our feet, give us something good to eat!"

"Exactly. Let's go!" said Skelly.

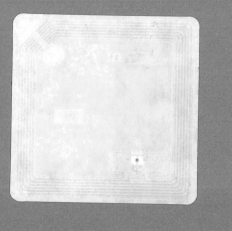

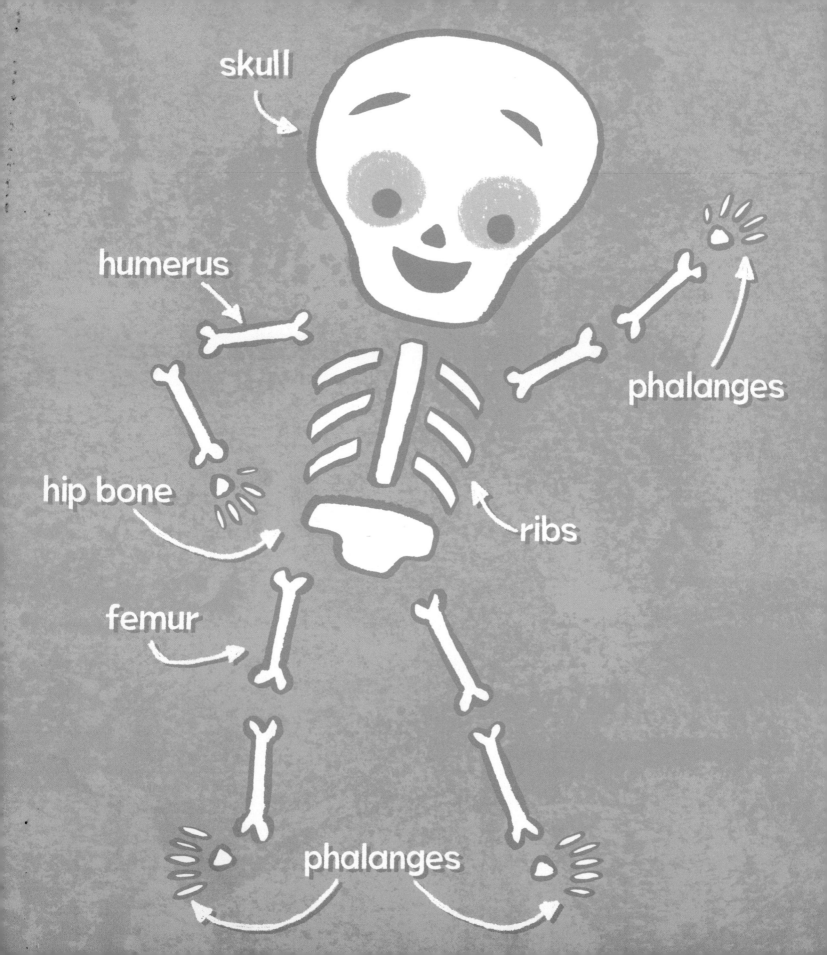